CHARLIE'S QUEST

Copyright © 2011 by Don Davis
First Edition – September 2011

ISBN
978-1-77097-033-5 (Hardcover)
978-1-77097-034-2 (Paperback)
978-1-77097-035-9 (eBook)

All rights reserved.

No part of this publication may be reproduced in any form, or by any means, electronic or mechanical, including photocopying, recording, or any information browsing, storage, or retrieval system, without permission in writing from the publisher.

Published by:

FriesenPress

Suite 300 – 852 Fort Street
Victoria, BC, Canada V8W 1H8

www.friesenpress.com

Distributed to the trade by The Ingram Book Company

Table of Contents

Foreword vii

CHAPTER 1
The Beginning 1

CHAPTER 2
From Bugs to Beds 7

CHAPTER 3
Gateway 15

CHAPTER 4
The Rehab 25

CHAPTER 5
Clubhouse Beach 41

CHAPTER 6
Pathways 55

CHAPTER 7
Parsing 63

CHAPTER 8
Crossroads 71

CHAPTER 9
The Library 79

Epilogue 87

Afterword 89

Acknowledgements 91

*This book is dedicated
to the miracle in my life,
my wife Nancy*

Foreword

This book was inspired by a real person who became a quadriplegic. I met "Charlie" (all characters' names were changed to protect their privacy) when, as a certified nursing orderly, I had the privilege of caring for him in the Manitoba Rehabilitation Hospital. I was seventeen years old at the time, and here I am, thirty-four years later, as acutely aware of his character as I was back then—so much so that I felt compelled to write this book. It's not a straightforward work of non-fiction, because I'd lost touch with Charlie some years ago. And then I heard that, sadly, he had died. All this was before I decided to write the book. Since I couldn't speak with him again about those long-ago events, I've taken the liberty of writing some sections more as a novelist might, putting myself in Charlie's place to imagine what he might have felt or thought or seen. But I've tried to stay faithful to my memories of Charlie, our deep friendship and the long conversations we had.

  Charlie was an incredible person: optimistic, appreciative, courageous; a man who looked beyond the surface of an issue and who would not let being a quadriplegic slow him down. I have never forgotten or lost my sense of what a privilege and an honor it was to work with Charlie, so my thanks to him for being a lifetime inspiration, and to all the other people I worked with who helped make this story come alive. I hope that Charlie's story will also be an inspiration to you, the reader.

Don Davis, August 2011

CHAPTER 1
The Beginning

It was the tenth of July and the night was jet black. A few stars looked out from behind low, foreboding clouds, and the white-notched highway stretched out in a never-ending strip of black ribbon. Music floated up from the truck's dashboard speakers, each note wrapped in the flow of heated air. Charlie rubbed the back of his hand across his eyes, trying to clear the film that was blurring his eyesight. He'd be finished this twenty-two-hour road trip in under an hour.

The road hiccupped in his vision. He shook his head, uncertain of what he'd seen. Something was tugging at the back of his mind. What was it? What was calling out to him? He shifted his attention back to the road. There it was again, a hiccup in the road. This time the hiccup became an alert. What was so important?

The search for clarity was slow and difficult and took every bit of his energy. Now he understood the warning. Charlie's eyes shot open. He had fallen asleep. The truck's front wheels were crossing the road's center line. As the sound of screaming tires filled his ears, the cement abutment of a bridge raced toward him.

At last, there was darkness, silence and no feeling.

When Charlie woke up, he felt as if he was floating on a cloud. Then all of a sudden, he started spiraling downward. A loud, rushing noise filled his ears, and a voice was screaming, begging for release. It sounded familiar, and he realized it was his. Light poured into his eyes. He heard a beeping sound, and a distant voice was saying his name. Who was speaking? He didn't recognize the voice.

A nurse appeared next to him. Peering over her glasses, she asked if he wanted something for the pain. Charlie uttered a hoarse "yes." She left the room for a few moments and returned with a needle, which she then inserted into his IV line, injecting its contents into his bloodstream. He felt a warm surge of relief spread across the tops of his shoulders, up to his neck and into his head. The beeping sound began fading into the background, and the screaming had stopped. A warm cloud floated up and embraced him. At last, comfort, darkness and peace.

Sounds drifted into his consciousness and drew him out of his sleep. The sounds were new and strange to him. As he rested with his eyes closed, he tried to understand the situation.

He was aware of four painful spots on his head, one on each side of his forehead and one on each side at the back of his head. He noticed that the pain became more intense the more he focused his attention on the spots. In the following days, Charlie would learn that these painful spots were four stainless steel bolts. Each bolt threaded through a stainless steel halo and tightened into his skull. A rope was attached to the center of the halo, and weights hung from its end. This apparatus formed the top portion of the traction system that was holding Charlie's body straight.

He opened his eyes. Right above him were two stainless steel rails that formed a semicircle. The two rails looked like half of a Ferris wheel minus the seats. What he was looking at was the top half of a circular bed called a Stryker unit. His eyelids became heavy with fatigue, and he floated back onto his cloud.

A warm face cloth wiped his face and woke him up, its moisture soothing his parched lips and cleansing his eyes and nose. The fresh, clean smell of lemon filled his nostrils. This simple act of having his face washed felt wonderful. He closed his eyes. Then he heard water splashing into a washbasin, and the sound of a cloth rubbing across skin. But he could no longer feel the facecloth rubbing his face or any other part of his body.

He heard his voice croaking out the question in his mind: "Nurse, is someone else bein' washed too?"

"No. you're in a private room. Are you enjoying your bed bath?"

Yeah, my face feels and smells nice and clean. But there's somethin' I don't get. Why can't I feel you washin' me below my shoulders?"

The splashing sounds stopped. "Charlie," said the nurse, "has the doctor spoken with you about your condition?"

"No, the docs haven't spoken to me."

"Can I ask you what's the last thing you remember before waking up in the hospital?"

"I remember drivin' my truck on the highway, listenin' to some music and then I woke up here."

Charlie opened his eyes. The nurse had a long, narrow face and she looked solemn behind her glasses. "Charlie, your truck hit a cement abutment and was destroyed. The rescue crew had to cut you out of your truck cab. You were dead on the scene, but they revived you. It's a miracle you're still alive. You're on a Stryker bed, which will hold you straight and keep you from moving. This will help your neck vertebrae heal. Once the vertebrae set, you'll be ready to go over to our rehabilitation unit for physiotherapy."

"I'm lookin' forward to that. How long will it be before I'm taken off this thing?"

"The doctors think it'll be somewhere between two and three weeks."

"So once I've done the physiotherapy, how long before I'm back on my feet?"

The nurse looked away. Then she turned back to Charlie. "I'm sorry, but it won't work out that way," she said softly. "The level of your spinal column injury is high, and because of that you're a quadriplegic."

"A quadri what?"

"You're a quadriplegic."

"What's a quadriplegic?"

"A quadriplegic is a person who's lost the use of his legs and the use of his arms and hands. Once you're off the Stryker unit you'll be custom fitted with a wheelchair to help you get around."

Charlie struggled to understand. "I thought you said this thing was gonna help heal my neck? If it's healin' my neck, why won't I be able to walk?"

"There's a limit to what the Stryker unit can do. It is helping to heal your vertebrae and some of the damage in your spinal cord. When you come off the Stryker, your next step will be sleeping on a standard hospital bed. As you continue to recover, you'll work out in both the physiotherapy and occupational therapy units.

Your progress in these areas will determine the types of tools you'll be fitted for to increase your independence."

The sound of the nurse's voice disappeared in the frantic buzz of thoughts swirling in Charlie's head—thoughts that swiftly turned into feelings, twisted through his body and headed for the pit of his stomach. Everything he had worked for, everything he had invested his time and money in, it all depended on him being able to walk and use his hands. His world was crumbling before his eyes, and all that he had been no longer existed.

"Leave me alone! Please stop washin' me now! Just leave me alone!"

"All right, Charlie, I'm going to cover you up to keep you warm. Don't be discouraged. The staff in the rehab unit is wonderful. You'll be amazed at how many things they'll be able to teach you. And the occupational therapy unit will help you expand your skills."

"I said leave me alone!"

Unable to cope with the magnitude of what he'd just heard, Charlie was sure the nurse had to be mistaken. This bed was going to heal his neck and he would walk out of the hospital. He stiffened his resolve against the onslaught of negative thoughts and feelings.

As he rested on the Stryker unit, he closed his eyes. He visualized himself driving his rig to pick up a load. He backed the unit up to the loading dock and shut the truck down. The cab door swung open and his hand grabbed hold of the vertical bar next to the door when he swung his body down to the pavement. He waved to the receiver as he walked to the loading dock with the bills of lading in his hands. Charlie tried to stop the images, but they would not stop. Now flashes of him doing his truck maintenance played across the screen in his mind. Then he saw himself walking into a new customer's office to discuss his company's services. He tried clamping his eyelids down to stop the images. This drew the skin on his forehead tight across the four stainless steel bolts, and made it feel as if each bolt was tearing his head open.

Pain replaced the images. Fatigue confused his thought processes.

The nurse and doctors had to be wrong about the extent of his injury. They were talking about a "life-changing event." He had heard about such a thing happening to other people, but it would not happen to him. He was sure he'd make a full recovery. As soon as he got off this Stryker unit, he'd commit all his energies to recovering completely.

Charlie did not realize that what he valued least would influence more people than he could imagine. He didn't realize that he was halfway through his life, but at the beginning of his quest.

CHAPTER 2
From Bugs to Beds

As I stood with an air-powered staple gun resting on my right hip, I heard the elevator door open and the pelt rack's wheels clatter over the elevator threshold. The seven other staplers and I would receive one bundle of pelts. Each bundle contained enough pre-cut matching pelts to make one fur coat or jacket. Our job was to match the pre-cut pieces of soaked fur to the corresponding wax-covered cardboard templates, and we had a template for each piece: collar, sleeves, back section and so on. Then the matching pieces of fur and templates were stapled on to the four-by-eight-foot plywood drying boards, so the pieces of fur would dry in the correct shape before being sewn together.

Over one hundred sewers sat across from the staplers' working area. The sewers were now stitching the pelts that the staplers had worked on the day before. This was the endless cycle. A punch clock recorded the precise time each worker came onto the pelt preparation floor. If one of the workers came in more than five minutes late, he or she would be docked fifteen minutes' pay.

It was 1967 and I was living in Winnipeg, Manitoba. My parents were in St. Louis, Missouri, where my father was a chaplain. I'd left school at fifteen and had worked as a busboy in my previous job for one dollar an hour. The menu at Cal's restaurant consisted of barbecued chicken and pizza, and it catered primarily to a lunchtime crowd of executives. I worked from nine in the morning to three in afternoon, and my monthly wage came to $132. By the time I paid for room and board at my aunt's place and bus fare, I didn't even have enough money to pay for my monthly cigarette needs (because it seemed everyone smoked in those days, and teenaged boys were no exception).

So when I'd seen the "Help Wanted" sign at Nieman's Furs, I was quick to inquire about hours of work and the hourly wage. They were paying $1.10 an hour and needed me for seven hours of work per day. That gave me $167 per month, which covered all of my basics: room and board, bus fare and cigarettes. I felt as if I had hit the jackpot.

I was lucky. During the first week of work, my supervisor took me under his wing and helped me develop good stapling technique. Each lunch hour all the staplers would go across the street and shoot billiards. I was on good terms with my supervisor and fellow workmates, and my monthly salary had gone up by 28 percent. As far as I was concerned things couldn't be better.

Work went well for quite a while but I started noticing that I was getting increasingly frustrated. My earnings were meeting my needs and my workmates were a good group. Regardless, my frustration continued to grow and I could not identify the source.

Television showed scenes of hippies carrying signs displaying the peace symbol. They spoke about love and making a better world to live in. These images and speeches strummed the strings of my idealistic core. Each day my restlessness grew, and each day I grew angrier without understanding the reason. There were no problems in my workplace, so the problem had to be in what I was doing. I needed to find a line of work that had more meaning.

Every chance I got, I read the newspaper's help-wanted section. And every day I failed to find any jobs that contributed to humanity's well-being. That is, I didn't find any jobs that had my experience and education listed as requirements. No one listed railway section man, floor cleaner, maintenance man, busboy or pelt blocker as qualifying experience. No one wanted a seventeen-year-old boy with a tenth-grade education working in a capacity that would influence the world. Everywhere I looked was a dead end.

Friends advised me to go back to school and finish my education. But I refused. When I had applied myself, the educational system had slapped me down and wiped out all the efforts I had made to improve my grades. I wouldn't throw myself into working in a system that failed to recognize hard work and quality classroom efforts.

Now I was working on the fifth floor of a sweatshop, caught in the double bind of stubbornness and idealism. But one day, while I worked on the pelts, a chance event would result in my finding a far more rewarding job. As our supervisor dropped a fresh bundle of pelts on my work area, I didn't realize the pelts were untreated and infested. When I picked up the first pelt, I didn't feel the tiny insects boring through the skin of my arms. I wiped the sweat from my forehead with my forearm, and they traveled across my face and neck and down my back. Within two days, I had to take time off work to deal with an infestation called scabies. I had to put ointment on all areas of my body, and change and wash my bedsheets and clothing each day. And I had to stay away from people until this infestation cleared up.

Near the end of my treatment period when I was clear of any infestation, my doctor allowed me the freedom of going out in public, and my aunt met me for lunch in a nearby restaurant. She had heard there was a position available at the Manitoba Rehabilitation Hospital, which was right across from the Children's Hospital of Winnipeg, where she worked as a nurse. She suggested I make an appointment with the head nurse responsible for hiring.

I was unable to go back to work for another two days, so I took my aunt's advice. I phoned the head of nursing at the Rehabilitation Hospital and booked an appointment. I used the time before the appointment to create a résumé that focused on my work experience and not on my education. I also highlighted my family's careers and the fact that they were involved in caring for people. When I got into the interview, I planned to speak with passion about my desire to help people. It was a long shot and it took guts, because I knew I didn't meet the educational and experience requirements.

"Don, how old are you?" asked Mrs. Sutter, the head of nursing, when we sat down for the interview.

"I'm seventeen years old," I answered.

A concerned furrow etched itself in her forehead. "Are you aware that applicants for this position must be eighteen years of age?"

"I didn't know that, but I'll be eighteen shortly."

This seemed to satisfy her and she moved onto the next issue. "I notice from your résumé that you haven't completed high school."

"Yes, but I plan on working toward my high school accreditation in the near future."

"This position doesn't require a high school certificate, but a higher grade level would be helpful."

Before she could scrutinize my résumé any further, I asked her a diversionary question. "Would you mind describing the position that's available? My aunt told me you had an opening. She works as a nurse across the street at the Children's Hospital."

Mrs Sutter's demeanor changed altogether. "You say your aunt is a nurse at the Children's Hospital? How long has she worked there?" What had been mild interest at the beginning of the interview now bordered on enthusiasm.

"She's been working at the Children's Hospital for fifteen years."

"Do you mind my asking what her name is?"

"Of course not. Her name is Bertha Elder."

"Don, the position we have available right now is for a nursing orderly. It involves caring for and observing patients assigned to you each day. That means you'll have to take care of most, if not all, of their personal needs. There is a six-month, in-house training program, which will teach you anatomy and physiology, plus sterile technique. We train you in sterile technique to enable you to catheterize your male patients." She paused and looked at me intently. "It takes a special kind of individual to do this work. Why do you think you could do it?"

"I live with my aunt and she's a ready source of information. Plus my mother's a registered nurse and a registered psychiatric nurse. I learned a lot from her just by living with her. She taught me the proper care of injuries and some knowledge of anatomy. She also cared for my grandmother in our home when she was dying from stomach cancer."

Mrs. Sutter nodded. "You've had more than average exposure to patient care. Don, if you accept the job, you'll be working on the fourth floor with amputees, paraplegics and quadriplegics. If you're interested, I'm willing to offer you this job. We would need you to start within two weeks. Now the starting salary is only $280 a month, but after satisfactory completion of a six-month probationary period, you'd be eligible for a nice monthly increase. Would you like time to think about it or can you give me your answer now?"

I was awestruck. First, I felt completely unqualified. Second, I never thought focusing on family members' jobs would do the trick. Third, $280 was close to a 70 percent increase in salary. There was only one possible answer.

"Thank you, Mrs. Sutter. I accept your offer."

"That's wonderful. Please report to my office in two weeks at 7:00 a.m. I'll take you through the hospital and give you a thorough orientation, and I'll also introduce you to most of the staff on your floor. Now one of the policies we have here at the Rehab, as we call it for short, is that staff members address each by their surname and not their first name. So at that time you'll notice that everyone will address you as Mr. Davis."

Her words barely registered. My mind was still taking it all in; I could hardly believe I'd landed a job helping people. What I didn't realize was the door that destiny had opened would have a major impact on two lives: Charlie's and mine.

CHAPTER 3

Gateway

Each time Charlie woke up he had to re-orient himself. The smell that exists in all hospitals filled his nostrils. The air also carried the sounds of staff working, elevator bells chiming, call bells ringing and more.

He had a never-ending flow of people in and out of his room at the Winnipeg General Hospital. Orderlies came in every two hours to turn him; technicians came to draw fresh blood samples; nurses checked his vital signs, hung new IV bags and gave him medications. Charlie had awakened in a new world. He had no idea that so many medical specialties existed. He saw neurologists, urologists, orthopedic surgeons, dermatologists, etiologists and many more. They were all doing their best to facilitate his recovery. At the end of each of their visits, he would ask the same question: "Am I improving, and if I am, what kind of improvement is taking place?"

It didn't matter whom he asked, no one could answer his question. Each time a doctor failed to answer his question, his frustration grew. He was part of a sophisticated health care system, but he felt as if he was the lead act in a three-ring circus. His healing process was incomplete. His progress was ambiguous. It seemed his life had become a series of "if"s. *If* his spinal column healed well, *if* his spinal cord damage wasn't too severe, *if* some of the breaks in his spinal cord were partial… Each of these "if"s held a different possibility of recovery for Charlie. It felt as if he had purchased a lottery ticket on his health. He would win some unidentified first level prize if one of his medical "if"s came in. If all of the medical "if"s came in, he would win the jackpot. What that jackpot was he didn't know.

For the moment, this was his life. He had two options: he could challenge the doctors for not answering his questions, or—the other, more practical option—he could accept the current ambiguity. He needed friends working on his case, not enemies.

In the midst of these thoughts, two orderlies came in and pulled the privacy curtain around his bed. They removed the linen sheet from his back and rubbed his skin with alcohol. They placed a fresh sheet on his back and put the top portion of the Stryker frame on top of the sheet. Then they quickly tightened two frame fasteners and wrapped two seat belts around both Stryker frames to keep Charlie from sliding out from between them when his body went into spasms. The first belt went around Charlie's torso at his elbows, and the second near his hips. When the orderlies finished rotating the frame, it had changed Charlie's scenery from floor tiles to ceiling tiles.

Charlie had placed all of his hopes on this Stryker unit. This circular traction device might help heal a critically important spinal cord fiber—the fiber that would make it possible for Charlie to move his neck or his hands. He didn't know what a reasonable expectation was. At this moment, all he could move were his jaw and facial muscles.

His previous life had consisted of fresh air, freedom of movement and a constant change of scenery. He took pride in being independent and not having to rely on anyone. The threads of independence were woven through the fabric of his being. He had made a one-man business successful, an achievement that required ingenuity. Each time he went out on the road, he had to make sure that all the necessary resources were on hand. It took foresight, planning and courage to travel the long highways alone. When Charlie took inventory of himself, self-reliance was at the top of his character profile.

But right now, he felt like a trapped animal. He was tied to a steel frame; the only movement he got each day was twelve rotations. It had been ten days since his accident, but it felt like an eternity.

As Charlie looked out the corner of his eye, he noticed he had a bedside table next to the Stryker unit. Two items sat on top of the table. The first was a glass of water with a bent straw in it. The second item that caught his attention was a handmade get-well card, lovingly fashioned by his three daughters, which his wife, Ruth, had brought in on her last visit. Even though he could see the card and glass of water, they were completely out of his reach. He would have to ask someone to give him a drink of water or show him the card. He would have to intrude on someone's time for such a simple thing. The pressure of being unable to move, of having to depend on everyone for everything, made him feel as if he would explode.

He glanced at his children's get-well card. The girls hadn't seen him yet. For that matter, even *he* hadn't seen himself yet. He had no idea what he looked like. Whenever the orderlies shaved him, they asked if he would like to see how good he looked. Looking in the mirror required more courage than he could muster. What would he see in the mirror? How would his children react when they saw him on the Stryker unit? Would they see a father, a provider, a protector, their source of strength and security? He didn't think so. In his current condition, he wondered what he had left to offer his wife and daughters. Before the accident, he could envision himself playing with the girls and taking them on a vacation. Now when he created an image of his family in his mind, all he saw was his wife and children interacting. He was unable to see himself anywhere in the family setting. It was as if the accident had erased him from his dreams—as if he had become invisible.

His large, six-feet-four-inch body lay motionless, held in place by the traction. Its stillness belied his intense internal battle. He was searching his mind for the tall, capable man who was the master of his domain at work and at home. Charlie struggled to hold onto that world. Every motionless moment was an attack on his pre-accident reality. The more he denied his current reality, the more warped and disconnected his life became. Time was blurring in Charlie's mind and it was losing shape and meaning. Days had ceased to exist by name and number and so were no longer a significant measurement tool. Noticing that he felt like a disconnected third party observing events from a distance, Charlie considered this idea of connection and disconnection.

Two separate worlds existed in his mind. One was the pre-accident world, which continued to exist and flow outside the hospital. Businesses continued to operate, trucks were still shipping orders, and companies continued to compete for business. Television networks broadcast images of this world, so he knew it existed, but he was no longer an active participant.

The other world existed within the walls of this hospital. In fact those walls contained a number of different-sized worlds, and the size of each depended on each patient's health. If a patient was in for a minor issue, that person's world consisted of the attending doctor and a few of the ward staff. If the patient had a more serious situation involving surgery, his or her world would consist of the attending doctor, the surgeon and perhaps a surgical nurse plus a few of the ward staff.

Charlie's hospital world was large because he was in critical condition. It consisted of his Stryker unit, numerous specialists, several nurses and the ward staff. The staff's goal was to help him heal and regain as much of his former physical abilities as possible. When he went over to the Rehabilitation Hospital, he wondered what his world would look like. He would have physiotherapy and occupational therapy. As large as he knew this seemed, it was suffocating and small compared to the pre-accident world he'd left outside the hospital.

If he really worked at it, he could imagine in his mind's eye a convergence between the Stryker unit and the outside world. If the Stryker unit did its job, he would be able to cross a bridge back to his pre-injury world. He knew that bridge was imaginary, but he prayed that what he'd imagined would become a reality. He wouldn't learn his degree of wholeness and brokenness, though, until he came off the Stryker.

He grew more uncertain and frustrated. Each morning the lights came on at 6:30 a.m., and the nurses gave him a bed bath and his medications. Even a simple task like taking pills required skills that Charlie no longer had. On one particular morning he'd choked on his medications—the pills lodged in his throat—and a quick-thinking nurse saved him by dislodging the pills. He'd been powerless to help himself. Struggling to move, he'd made a feeble attempt to help, his reward for this invisible gesture an excruciating spasm of pain that ran everywhere he could feel. Even a newborn baby could have done more.

With the pills cleared from his throat, he would live again. Once more, he'd avoided death's grip. First, the ambulance attendants had revived him at the accident scene, and now the nursing staff had saved his life. Why?

He ground his teeth together. On one hand, he felt protected, as if there was some unknown reason that he should live. On the other hand, why should he live if he couldn't do anything? But it felt as if he couldn't die even if he wanted to. If his situation wasn't so depressing it would almost be laughable.

The nurses had pinned his call cord next to his mouth, but Charlie couldn't notify the nurses if he needed help. To pull the cord, he'd need to move his head—and he had his head locked in position by a stainless steel halo. They had moved him into a room next to the nursing station and told him to call if he needed help. This wouldn't work either. His neck injury was so high that he was incapable of inhaling extra air into his lungs. Without the additional air, shouting for help was impossible!

"My God," Charlie thought, "I'm completely helpless. If I get into trouble I could die in here and no one would know. I can't call out for help. I can't move."

It was on the night following the pill incident, in a quiet dark room, that Charlie's truth came crashing down around him. The implications of what being completely paralyzed meant hit him hard. An air-blocking form of terror started rising in his chest; it rose into his throat and he felt as though he was suffocating. He started to gasp for air.

Because of the break in his neck, the muscles in Charlie's chest couldn't expand to allow more air into his lungs, and his diaphragm wouldn't respond and inhale more air. Since his accident, Charlie had been getting just enough air to breathe. Now, caught in the middle of a horrifying panic attack, he was extremely short of air. He began to feel faint, and a haze started forming in his mind, blurring the terrifying images that flashed through it. Darkness swept in on him. Charlie was convinced he had come to the end of his life. The last image he remembered was of falling into a black, formless void.

About an hour later, two orderlies came into Charlie's room to turn him. When they woke him up, Charlie didn't believe what was happening. A feeling of wonder spread over him as they removed his blankets and belts; it felt as if he was getting yet another chance at life. A mixture of fear and optimism rose inside him. The orderlies, unaware of the complex set of emotions and thoughts swirling through him, went through the steps to rotate Charlie and the frames 180 degrees so that he was now facing the floor. After tightening the two belts around his body, they left him and moved on to the next room. Neither one of the orderlies was aware that Charlie was on the verge of an emotional, intellectual and spiritual awakening that would change the course of his life.

Charlie had lost consciousness an hour earlier, believing that his life was over. Now his mind and heart were racing. He was spiraling out of control. One minute he was wondering what he had to live for, and the next he found himself grateful and excited that he was still alive. Now, for the first time in nearly two weeks, he was looking life in the face. At this moment, he wasn't thinking about his many limitations. He was aware that he was alive, and that he wanted to be alive. Where was he going? Where would he go? What would he do? What value was he to anyone? None of this mattered, because he was excited about being alive, and there *had* to be something for him to do. How many wake-up calls did he need to accept that he had an important role to play?

Tears began falling from his face: tears that expressed the terrible emptiness that had filled him since his accident; tears that spoke of the shame he felt for letting himself get into this situation. His tears hitting the floor sounded like the beating of a drum, announcing his fear to the world. Tears were flowing like rivers, filled with images of his many personal losses. As the tears fell, Charlie was aware that he was also opening the gates to his anger and frustration. He felt a boiling rage building up in him—a rage that he'd been unaware of until now. He condemned himself for failing, and raged against his body for failing him when he needed it. He raged against the doctors, whose job it was to heal him, for failing him. There were so many failures, so many losses.

As the hot tears flowed out, smothering toxic emotions flowed out of him too. They'd locked his mind, heart and soul in a dark world where he'd been incapable of seeing images of his future. Almost silently, Charlie continued the work of releasing his inner pain. Now cleansed of self-condemnation and judgment, he was taking the first steps on his new road into the future. Charlie had begun the most important phase of his internal healing.

As the intensity of his emotions abated, Charlie was amazed at the peace that was moving in behind his tears. A wonderful sense of wholeness filled his inner core. As the final drops of grief and anger left him, he was aware a transition had begun. It had started when the pill got stuck and he thought he was dying. He had unconditionally accepted his broken state and released himself to death. At that moment, he had opened a gateway to his mind, heart and spirit. The second critical step took place when the orderlies arrived to turn him. When he realized that he was alive, his true feelings about living had risen into his conscious mind. He wanted to live; he was thrilled. And when he released his grief and anger, he stepped through a gateway of opportunity.

He relaxed on the Stryker frame. A new sense of calmness came over him, a calmness that had escaped him these past weeks. The sound of the nurses' voices flowed into his room. For some inexplicable reason, the sound no longer grated on his nerves. Perhaps it was because he no longer believed his well-being depended solely on the nurses. He closed his eyes and found himself muttering the words, "Thank you, God."

At that precise moment, he could have sworn he received an unspoken assurance that God had been waiting for him to utter these words from his heart. A warm and comforting sensation filled him. He had experienced this feeling once, many years before. As a teen, he had attended a conference. The speaker had asked the audience if they were tired of carrying an unbearable load of anger and fear. Charlie felt as if the speaker was talking directly to him. Was he tired of feeling shame over failures in his life? Would he like to be free from these burdens forever? At that moment Charlie decided to accept Jesus as his savior, and he walked forward to the words of Charles Elliott's song:

"Just as I am, though tossed about,

With many a conflict, many a doubt,

Fights and fears within, without,

O Lamb of God, I come."

Charlie knew that everything was going to be all right. He let himself drift into a deep sleep that renewed his body, mind and spirit as the song's words played repeatedly in his head.

CHAPTER 4

The Rehab

A bright shaft of sunlight blazed through a small crack in Charlie's curtains and fell on his children's get-well card. He studied the image they had drawn. Today he saw something different. Was it because it was highlighted by the sunlight, or was it because he had a new outlook on life? The card showed his wife and three girls playing in front of their home. Before today, he had failed to notice he was sitting in the middle of the group in his wheelchair. Charlie had missed his children's message of unconditional love: they had accepted him in a wheelchair. While he had condemned himself for his shortcomings, his three daughters drew him into the center of their lives. They didn't consider him unreachable or foreign; he was still their dad. Tears of joy ran down his face.

Another thought struck him as he experienced this love-filled moment. He was experiencing life through a different lens filter. It was as if a dark, impenetrable veil no longer obstructed his view of life. He saw life more clearly, more completely. He felt much lighter in spirit, free from the weight of anger and self-condemnation.

Because his fear and anger had blocked his rational thought processes, he had, he now realized, adopted a rigid way of thinking. But now he knew he had to move forward, and for that he needed his creative childhood mind working—a fresh way of looking at things, without bias. And he needed confidence, humor and the mind of an explorer.

During the afternoon, a group of doctors appeared in his room. They had good news: the next morning he was going to be transferred from the General Hospital to the Rehabilitation Hospital. They had reviewed his recent X-rays, which showed good healing progress in Charlie's neck. So he would stay on the Stryker unit for one more week, then transfer to a normal hospital bed. Physiotherapists at the Rehab hospital would assess him on his arrival, and their assessment would determine the scope of Charlie's therapy program.

The next morning a porter appeared at his door to transport him to the Rehab. Charlie traveled through a long underground tunnel connecting the two hospitals, with bright fluorescent lights all along its ceiling. As Charlie moved through the tunnel, the lights and their moving reflections bouncing off the Stryker unit's polished stainless steel bars, creating a visual extravaganza. He felt like a kid traveling through a circus midway.

The rehab unit was the next step of his quest. Whatever abilities he developed during his physiotherapy would increase his future job opportunities. His job prospects depended on the work capacity he had to offer.

Because the big Stryker unit didn't fit into a semi-private room, the porter put him in a private room across from the nurses' station. The rehab unit staff were knowledgeable and pleasant; they explained where the various departments were and gave Charlie the name of his physiotherapist.

This was my first opportunity to meet Charlie. Although I'd never seen a Stryker unit before, Paul, the other orderly I worked with, had previous experience with Strykers and assured me he'd explain everything. Paul and I had quickly become good friends, and whenever we met a new patient, we had three objectives. Our first goal was to make each patient feel comfortable and confident about our knowledge. The second was to make sure the patient knew we were an important part of his or her rehabilitation program, and were always available to answer questions. Our third goal was to create an enjoyable working atmosphere, even though we worked hard.

When the nurses and other support staff had finished meeting Charlie, Paul and I introduced ourselves.

I spoke for the two of us. "Good morning, Charlie. I'm Don and next to me is my fellow orderly and friend Paul. We're pleased to have you as a member of the fourth floor and we both look forward to working with you. You've had a lot of information coming at you today. Do you have any questions?"

Charlie smiled and said, "Hey, I'm pleased to meet you both. Now that I know your names, I'll make sure I ask for one of you. And no, I don't have any questions, but I can tell you one thing—I'm impressed with the Rehab staff. You're all very friendly and efficient, and I'm really lookin' forward to gettin' started on my physiotherapy program. Thanks for stoppin' and introducin' yourselves."

"Well," Paul said, "let us know if you need anything and we'll make sure we take care of you."

As Paul and I walked away from Charlie's room we were both impressed. New quadriplegics are usually dealing with negative emotions: they're angry or depressed. Charlie stood out because he'd shown such genuine enthusiasm and pleasure when we met him. No other patient with his level of disability could match his optimism and genuine gratitude for even the smallest thing others might take for granted.

As a result, I was drawn to Charlie. He was easy to talk to, and I found myself telling him all sorts of things. One day as I was bathing him, he mentioned he had trouble sleeping. I asked if he'd heard of meditation. Some of my hippie friends had been talking about it.

"It's a way of emptying and calming your mind," I said. Charlie was intrigued so I told him what little I knew, and he said he'd like to try it.

… …

At 9:00 p.m., the lights went out. Charlie had decided he wanted to use his evenings, after lights out, to do one of two things: If he'd had a tiring day, meditation would be his first choice. If he felt fresh and not fatigued, he'd use the evening for exploring new ideas for his future.

Since he was physically tired from that day's activities, even though he thought it had been a wonderful day, he decided to try meditation. He closed his eyes and let his mind wander. But he noticed that his mind didn't simply go into a relaxed form of meditation. The events of the day had stimulated his brain. When he closed his eyes, an endless number of thoughts and images hit the screen in his mind in a whirling blur. It was impossible to shut his head down. Charlie hadn't anticipated any trouble achieving a state of meditation. He thought it would be a simple process of closing his eyes and descending into a quiet, dark and blissful place. But no matter how hard he tried, meditation wasn't going to happen that night. He decided he needed more information about meditation techniques before he tried again.

As fatigue finally overtook him, his eyes closed and he drifted off to sleep. He loved sleep because it took him to a world where anything was possible. He could walk on the beach with his wife, run in the playground with his children, play baseball with his friends, drive his truck through the provinces and do any other activity he could imagine.

Just before his midnight Stryker turning, Charlie discovered that almost all of the patients' calm daytime exteriors collapsed in the dark isolation of the night. He was enjoying a sound sleep when he heard a blood-curdling scream. It shocked his senses and startled him into full alertness. The quiet atmosphere returned and Charlie wondered if he had dreamed the terrifying scream. It had been a woman's voice, and it sounded as if someone had attacked her or something horrible had happened to her. He strained to hear more and caught the soft sound of a woman sobbing from down the hallway. As the pitch of her cries rose and fell, one of the nurses got up from the nursing station and walked quickly down the hall. He heard the nurse speaking in low, reassuring tones, and the sobbing gradually ebbed and ultimately ceased. Charlie wondered if the woman had hurt herself or had a nightmare.

The following morning I brought Charlie some fresh towels, a washcloth and a basin in preparation for his bed bath and said, "Good morning, Charlie, did you have a good night's sleep?"

Charlie's reply surprised me. "Actually I didn't. Last night I woke up to the sound of a woman screamin'. It scared me a lot and I had trouble settlin' my mind and goin' back to sleep. Would you have any idea who it was?"

"No, Charlie, I don't. No one said anything in this morning's staff briefing about someone having a problem during the night. But I should tell you that the hospital has a strict policy concerning patient confidentiality. Staff can't discuss one patient's issues with another patient. This way you know we're all committed to protecting your privacy."

Charlie took this in and then he said, "That makes sense, and to be honest it makes me feel better knowin' the hospital has that policy."

As I was giving Charlie his bed bath, I was thinking again that there was something special about this man. "Charlie," I said, "would you mind me visiting with you whenever I have some spare time?"

"I'd like that," he replied. "I'm sure you can help me understand other hospital policies. Plus I'd love to learn more about the various departments, and anythin' else you think might be helpful for me to know."

"I'd enjoy talking about the Rehab," I said, using the last of the towels to dry him off. "And I think you and I would both get something out of sharing thoughts and ideas, so whenever I get some time I'll drop in and see how you're doing."

As I left Charlie, I saw Richard wheeling his chair toward Charlie's room. Richard was a paraplegic currently in the Rehab Hospital for a trial treatment program. He was also the unofficial new patient greeter. He made sure he introduced himself to all the new patients, found out what had happened to cause their injuries and provided all of the ward's latest gossip. I knew Charlie would get his answers about the screaming patient.

… …

Charlie was lying on his back on the Stryker frame when he heard a voice coming from below his line of sight.

"Hi, my name is Richard—this is the first chance I have had to introduce myself. What's your name?'

"Hi, I'm Charlie. This Stryker frame keeps me from bein' able to sit up and see you."

"It's not a problem. I've been a paraplegic for twelve years. My car spun out control on a gravel road and rolled into the ditch—I'm lucky that I lived through the accident. What happened to you?"

"I was drivin' an eighteen wheeler and fell asleep at the wheel. The nurses told me that my truck crashed into a cement abutment and that's how I broke my neck. They also told me that I was dead on the scene and that the ambulance attendants saved my life. I'm a quadriplegic now. I'll be off this frame by the end of next week. Do you mind if I ask you a question, Richard?"

"No, not at all, fire away."

"Last night I was woken up by a woman screamin'. Did you hear that too?"

"Sure did. She screams on a regular basis at night time, but you'll get used to it."

"Is she in pain or hurtin' herself?"

"No, she's not in pain. She has recurring nightmares. I talked to her about it one day, after the first time her screams scared the pants off me. She's a quadriplegic too. She and her husband were out for a drive in their car and they got into an accident. A fully loaded semi-trailer pulled out in front of their vehicle. Their car went right under the truck's trailer. The trailer sheared the roof of the car right off. She ducked, but still broke her neck. When she ducked, she looked over at her husband in time to see him decapitated. She keeps reliving that moment in her dreams and that's why she screams."

Charlie sucked in air at the image this story had burned into his memory. What a horrible experience for her to relive repeatedly.

"How many quadriplegics are there on our floor?" Charlie asked.

"Right now there are four quadriplegics, three men counting yourself and one woman."

"How many paraplegics are there?"

"Six paraplegics, five men counting myself and one woman."

"Are there any other quadriplegics or paraplegics that had an unusually bad experience like our screaming patient?"

"One of our quadriplegics, Jerry, had his neck broken by his best friend. And one of our paraplegics—name of Matthew—he went through a rough time. He's a twenty-seven-year-old engineer. Life was great for him and his beautiful young fiancée until she broke off their engagement. Matthew couldn't take the rejection so he went home and took his twenty-two caliber rifle out and shot himself. But he didn't succeed in killing himself. All he did was sever his spinal cord with the bullet. He stays awake late at night and battles a serious case of depression."

Richard paused for a moment while a noisy stretcher rolled down the hallway outside the door.

"We also have an eighteen-year-old female paraplegic," Richard continued. "Her name is Jenny. She and a group of her friends were at their high school prom. When it came time to go home, the only ride available to her was with a group that were all drunk. She's a non-drinker and the driver was totally plastered. He lost control of the car and it rolled into a ditch. She was the only person injured. Now she's a paraplegic, trying to give up her past hopes and rewriting her future. Where's the justice in that?"

Charlie sighed. "There's no rhyme or reason to the things that happen in this world. I look forward to meetin' you again when I'm off this thing, so I can see your face."

"Yeah, that'll be great. I'll see you later. It's been a slice."

After Richard had gone, Charlie realized that all the people in this particular hospital were dealing with a "life-changing event." Each patient was battling his or her own unique, difficult situation. All faced the reality that they'd never be capable of doing the things that were possible prior to their accident.

The time slipped by as Charlie rested on the Stryker unit. Before he realized it, the lights went off, signaling the end of another day. Once again, he chose meditation as his focus for the evening. This time he took deep breaths, as deep as his limited respiratory system would allow. He did this repeatedly until he felt himself relaxing. He looked for a quiet and peaceful place in his mind. Again, his mind was a pandemonium of whirling images and thoughts. But this time it seemed the images and thoughts were becoming clearer, and he could even identify the odd image as it flew by. Although he couldn't hold onto it for any length of time, even a small gain was encouraging. Content that he had done as much as possible, he drifted into a peaceful sleep. Each night he alternated his routine between meditation and idea generation. This went on for six days.

The following day was a special day, and Charlie's excitement was palpable. The bedside clock numbers clicked the minutes away. Today he was more sensitive to sounds than usual, and he wondered if his enthusiasm was amplifying his senses.

A smile filled his broad face. This action drew the skin on his head tight, creating searing pain around the four stainless steel bolts screwed into his skull. Without conscious effort, an image of Ruth playing with their three girls filled his mind, and this image drove the discomfort into the background. He thought about that for a moment and decided he'd use this experience in the future. Whenever he experienced pain, he would displace it by focusing on an image that contained intense emotions. His visualization skills would be a useful asset. He was determined that nothing was going to spoil this day and that he was going to savor every minute.

He looked out the corner of his eye; his clock's crimson numbers indicated it was 5:30 a.m. This was the first time he had awakened before the nurses came in. He closed his eyes and tried to go back to sleep, but images of his anticipated freedoms flashed through his mind. His excitement was fueling his brain, and the result was rapid and uncontrolled imagery. He opened his eyes, hoping this would stop, or at least slow, the dizzying number of images. Looking out the corner of his eye, he saw it was now 5:33 a.m. In fifty-seven minutes, the nurses would be coming into his room.

What he was feeling this morning was similar to what he had experienced when he'd first dated Ruth. She had expanded his experience of life from the moment he met her, and he had become a new man. She always generated the same response in him: positive, creative energy. The thought of coming off the Stryker unit was also flooding his mind with creative and positive energy. He knew he needed to channel this force, so he closed his eyes and let memories of times with his wife flow through his mind. A warm, serene flow of energy replaced the frenetic images. Eventually he drifted into peaceful sleep.

"Good morning Charlie, how are you?" said Sheila, one of the unit's nurses, as she turning on the lights in his room.

"Sheila, I'm glad to see you. Today I come off this thing."

"Yes we were talking about you in our morning staff meeting. You're to come off the Stryker unit at noon today. We don't get many patients on Stryker units, so the senior nursing staff and the residents are coming to observe how a Stryker is set up, how it works and how a patient is taken off one. Dr. Quinn will be conducting the training session."

Sure enough, at noon Dr. Quinn, stocky and blond-haired, walked off the elevators and onto the fourth floor. A combination of lab coats, white nurse's uniforms, starched white nurse's hats and green surgical outfits thronged the hallway outside Charlie's room. In the low, mumbling voices of the waiting audience, an unmistakable excitement could be heard. This amplified Charlie's own rising excitement.

As Dr. Quinn approached Charlie's room, a path opened up through the waiting trainees and closed behind him as he proceeded through the group, which followed him into Charlie's room. There Dr. Quinn explained the numerous functions of a Stryker unit, describing how each change in its setup allowed medical staff different options for providing care without endangering the patient or the healing process. Then he asked one of the residents to stand at the foot end of the Stryker frame.

After giving some brief directions, Dr. Quinn and the resident began the process of disconnecting Charlie from the frame. First they removed the weights at both his head and feet; then the resident untied the corset wrapped around Charlie's lower body. Next, Dr. Quinn removed the rope from the stainless steel halo. Then, producing a tool from his pocket, the doctor loosened off each of the stainless steel bolts, bit by bit, from Charlie's head. A nurse assisted him by holding the halo steady until the bolts were all out of Charlie's skull. As soon as the halo was clear of his head, Dr. Quinn fastened a cloth-covered collar around Charlie's neck for support. The last step was to remove the two belts from Charlie's torso.

At that point, Dr. Quinn asked the assembled group if anyone had additional questions and proceeded to answer a few questions from the nurses and residents.

Suddenly a hoarse voice rose from the frame of the Stryker unit. "Doc, how much healin' has taken place in my neck as a consequence of my bein' on this thing?" Charlie asked.

Dr. Quinn looked like a deer caught in car headlights.

"That's a good question, Charlie. The X-rays show satisfactory healing of the cervical spine break. Because this has been achieved, the spinal column is now stable enough to allow you to be transferred off the Stryker unit to a hospital bed."

"What other things have healed and what does it mean to my recovery?"

"At the time of your accident, you severely damaged your cervical spinal cord. We hoped that more of the spinal cord would self-repair while you were on the Stryker unit. We're pleased to see improvement in your respiration during this period." The doctor paused here and cleared his throat. "But I am sorry to say this is the only gain we've been able to identify. Physiotherapy and occupational therapy will determine if any additional functional gains may be made in your upper extremities."

"What does that mean?"

Dr. Quinn looked at Charlie the way a trucker looks at a load of cattle and continued: "What it means is you'll be able to breathe on your own and won't require any additional assistance. It also means that it's unlikely you'll have even slight improvement in the movement of your arms."

"But I can't move my arms at all!"

"I regret that science has not advanced far enough for us to do anything more for you. Wait and see how things work out in physiotherapy. We've seen some surprising gains during these sessions. Now, if there are no additional questions I'll bid you a good day."

With that last comment, Dr. Quinn pivoted on one foot and left the room, unaware he had manhandled Charlie's emotions. With that one flippant comment about the limitations of today's medicine, he had dashed Charlie's hopes and dreams. The residents and nurses followed Dr. Quinn out, all of them oblivious to the utter insensitivity that had taken place. The only people remaining in the room were Charlie, Paul and I.

Charlie lay motionless on the Stryker frame. He had invested all his hopes in the possibility of making real progress on the Stryker unit. Deep in his heart he knew he had been unrealistic in hoping to gain partial-to-complete mobility in his legs and arms.

Nausea swept over him. This slap of reality left Charlie battered and numb. It would take time for him to accept the verdict he had been given. It would take time for the hurt to soften, to accept this new truth. Charlie finally became aware that I was talking to him.

"Charlie we've got a surprise for you. We're moving you into a four-person ward. Two of the men in this ward are quadriplegics. They'll probably tell you about their experiences, and we're sure they'll have some useful ideas on how to do things."

We wrapped the two seat belts around Charlie and the Stryker frame and pushed it into the hospital hallway. A short trip down the hall and we were in a large hospital room with four beds. After rolling the Stryker unit alongside an empty bed, we undid the belts and asked Charlie if he was ready. He had barely said yes and we'd transferred him to the bed. As Paul pushed the Stryker frame out of the room and it disappeared through the door, Charlie smiled and whispered "Goodbye."

Then we took the two belts and once again wrapped them around him at both thigh and chest level. These would remain in place until we were sure that Charlie's body spasms wouldn't throw him out of bed.

Charlie pushed the conversation with the doctor out of his mind. He was going to try to enjoy this part of the day. He was about to experience his first freedom since being admitted to the hospital. He turned to us and asked us to raise the head of his bed. As the head of the bed rose, he saw his roommates for the first time. He also noticed the doorway next to his bed. All of these images were new and huge. No longer a prisoner of the Stryker frame, he was regaining some of his lost world. Once again, he had a 180-degree view of his environment. This was Charlie's first tangible gain, and it felt good. He was also a member of a four-person hospital room, so he now belonged to a group. His time of isolation was over. Perhaps these men would share how they were dealing with their situation. How had they figured out their new role in the world? He knew that having someone to talk to was going to be a vast improvement.

CHAPTER 5
Clubhouse Beach

Clubhouse Beach is the most popular place to bathe and sunbathe at Victoria Beach. At one end of the beach an outcrop of water-worn boulders extends into the lake like a huge breakwater. Other boulders are randomly scattered around the beach area, and seagulls swoop down over the water to snatch their lunchtime catch. A consistent gentle breeze keeps the bathers and tanners refreshed as they walk on the fine sand. Families come here to rest, tan, and play with their children; young couples set their towels together and lie close to each other.

As teenagers, Charlie and Ruth would drive around, looking for a friendly, comfortable area to spend time together. Clubhouse Beach was one of their favorite spots. Charlie's wavy dark brown hair bracketed a broad, good-looking masculine face; tall, tanned and muscled, he cut an imposing figure. Ruth had long blonde hair that framed her heart-shaped face, and her diminutive five-foot body created the perfect visual contrast when she and Charlie walked next to one another.

Charlie had always been quiet and awkward with members of the opposite sex, and had hoped that he'd find a young woman like Ruth who could accept his awkwardness. His main areas of interest in high school were trucks, fishing and football. Charlie's love for working on trucks would serve him well when he started his trucking business and, meanwhile, his tall, rugged form was an impressive deterrent to the other team's offensive players when they tried to sack his quarterback. Ruth loved coming out to watch him play football. She had an athletic side to her too and enjoyed tossing a football around with Charlie. She was smart girl, and Charlie loved talking to her about anything.

Today Charlie, Ruth and their daughters Christina, Angela and Kara were walking past the front of Victoria Beach's Community Clubhouse. Christina was their oldest child, an attractive fourteen-year-old brunette who excelled in academics, loved children and enjoyed gymnastics. A strange thing had happened to Christina in the past two months. She had managed to acquire more knowledge than the combined knowledge and experience of both her mother and father. Christina was quick to point out their lack of knowledge on every possible occasion. Their middle child, Angela, was a striking blonde-haired girl, much like her mother. Going on twelve, she found school boring and had recently discovered that boys were not the total weirdos she'd thought they were. Kara, their precocious six-year-old, was charming and flighty and had an adventurous streak. All three girls were delightfully different, and each one had her dad wrapped around her little finger.

The clubhouse was a one story, multi-purpose, all-wooden building. Charlie and his family attended non-denominational church services there on Sunday mornings. On Tuesdays, a travelogue was hosted by one of the summer residents. They brought slides and provided commentary on the highlights of their trip. Wednesday and Thursday nights were movie nights, and Charlie's daughters attended the G-rated movies. A disc jockey hosted dances on both Friday and Saturday nights. Although Charlie's two oldest girls were too young to attend the dances, that never stopped them from bringing up the subject. They'd complain that they had nothing to do and how unfair it was because "everybody" else was allowed to go to the dance.

As the family came to the southern corner of the clubhouse, they turned and walked onto Clubhouse Beach. This was their favorite spot for sunbathing, playing catch with a Frisbee, body surfing and swimming. The sand on this beach was so fine their feet sank until each foot was completely covered.

The waves were higher at this part of Clubhouse Beach which made it ideal for body surfing. The girls spent hours jumping in front of each wave and sliding down its face. Charlie and Ruth loved watching each of the girls as they completed what they called their "championship rides," shrieking with delight. The seagulls rose and fell on the winds that were always present at Clubhouse Beach. Charlie got lost in some train of thought as he watched the birds soar and descend. Stretched out on a towel next to him, Ruth absorbed the warm summer sun. Charlie looked up toward the sun, and its intense light made him clamp his eyes tight and turn away.

When he opened them again, he realized he had been dreaming and he was now looking into the bright light over his hospital bed. For a few moments, he was stunned into silence. What had been so real, so touchable, had just been a dream—a dream that contained many precious past experiences and activities shared first as a teenage couple and as a family. As the images of the dream drifted away, the hard reality of where he was took over. Charlie thought about the benefits of escaping into dream worlds. They allowed him to live the life that his accident had taken away. At anytime he could slip into sleep, call upon the dream gods and live a fulfilling life. But then he thought of how empty he felt on waking up from his Club House Beach dream. Instinctively he knew that trying to recapture his past life through dreams was a dangerous idea. All he could hope for was an ever-increasing sense of loss. Not only would he suffer feelings of loss in his real world, he would double that sense of loss by tapping into a dream life. No, this was an idea he would not give conscious support to. He willed himself to return to his new reality.

As a newcomer to the ward, Charlie didn't initiate conversation with anyone until he got to know them better. Besides, his first few days in his new room were busy ones. He had an interview with his physiotherapist, he completed his patient profile with the ward clerk, and then he started right into his physiotherapy program. He had committed his evenings to considering future job opportunities that would be appropriate for him, but the problem was he wasn't sure how to approach the entire subject. One approach would be to identify his areas of greatest interest, and then look for related jobs. Another approach would be to look at jobs he had held and see what kind of skills he had developed in them. The job descriptions that listed matching skills would be the right jobs for him. The last possible approach would be to examine his educational background to see if he had acquired key knowledge. He had attended numerous private educational programs designed to help him set-up a company, organize it and make it successful.

Three possible approaches, but none appeared to stand out as better than the others.

His roommates were within his age group and each had a different work history. In the bed across from Charlie lay Anthony, a quadriplegic who hadn't spoken to anyone since Charlie had transferred into this ward. That was the extent of Charlie's knowledge of Anthony. Jerry was in the bed next to Anthony. He was apparently a partial quadriplegic, though Charlie wasn't sure what that meant. He would ask when he finally got into a conversation with Jerry. Across from Jerry and on Charlie's right-hand side was Harvey. Harvey was a paraplegic and that was all Charlie knew about him. He hoped to learn a great deal from his roommates— what kind of work they did, how they'd chosen that line of work and so on.

Between Charlie's physiotherapy program, his roommate's physiotherapy programs and their occupational therapy training, he didn't get a chance to talk with them until the weekend. Patients' therapy and training programs shut down on weekends. On Saturday Charlie had been fed breakfast and had his bed bath. As soon as this was finished, Jerry got into his wheelchair and came over to his bedside. Charlie watched him wheel his chair. Both of Jerry's large wheels were fitted with rubber-covered metal rods, about four inches in length and eight inches apart. Jerry's hand movement was limited and he couldn't grasp the wheel rim to propel his wheelchair. He used the "V" formed by his thumb and index finger to catch the rubber covered rods. It worked well as a means of propelling his wheelchair forward. Its brake locks performed two functions. The first was to bring his chair to a complete stop. The second allowed Jerry to put on one of his brakes only, which would make his chair turn one way or another. Charlie was fascinated by this custom-designed wheelchair. None of the patients he had seen in physiotherapy or in the halls had this unique design.

"Hi, I'm Jerry, and I'm a partial quadriplegic. What's your name?"

"My name is Charlie and I'm a full quadriplegic. I don't have any use of my hands, arms or legs. I'm curious about your wheelchair. I think the rubber extensions on your wheels are a pretty clever way for you to be mobile. Were you a full quadriplegic at the beginnin' and over time you healed enough to become a partial quadriplegic?"

"I wish I could tell you that." Jerry looked at Charlie sympathetically. "But the break in my neck didn't go all the way through my spinal cord. The benefit is the wheelchair freedom I have. I have partial use of my hands and seventy percent use of my arms. Do you mind telling me how you became a quadriplegic?"

"Sure thing." And Charlie told his story again.

"Ouch," exclaimed Jerry, "I hope physiotherapy helps you regain some of your hand function. Sometimes they even get back some neck rotation. It all depends on whether or not you have a complete, through-and-through spinal cord break. If you have unbroken nerve fibers, they sometimes reactivate the areas they control. It doesn't happen often, but it still happens sometimes. I'll keep my fingers crossed for you."

"Thanks Jerry, I appreciate the information you've given me and your encouragement. Do you mind me askin' how you ended up this way?"

"Well, my story has other characters involved—you see, I'm not the reason my neck is broken. I used to work in the mines up north before my injury. Here, I have a photo of me from that time." Jerry went over to his bedside table and pulled out a photo for Charlie to see.

Charlie saw a picture of a tall man with no shirt on. He was tanned and muscled.

Jerry continued, "When I finished working at the mines, I had a lot of money saved up, and I decided I deserved a break from work. I'd been working non-stop in the mines for five years. I was over six feet tall and with the muscles I had developed from the hard work, few people dared to challenge me. I met a fellow, his name was Jim, and over time, he and I became best friends. We went to a house party hosted by people we knew. Both Jim and I got into our cups that night. When I drink, I stay the same easygoing person. When my former friend Jim drinks, he goes through a complete personality change and gets a mean edge to him. He's nowhere near my height and a lot weaker. About halfway through the night Jim came over to me and challenged me to a fight. I laughed it off, told Jim to sober up and have a good time. When I walked away from him, he came up from behind me, wrapped his arm around my neck, and gave it a solid jerk backwards. All I remember hearing as I passed out was the snapping sound of my neck."

Jerry stopped at this point, wheeled back to his night table and put the photo of his former self away in the drawer. Then he rolled back to Charlie's bedside. His face looked grim.

"I made a promise to myself. I have a specially equipped car that I can drive anywhere. When I get out of the Rehab, I'm going to stake out Jim's place. I've got a twenty-two caliber rifle and I can rest the barrel on my side view mirror to hold it steady. When

Jim comes out, I'm going to take him down for good. He will *not* get away from me, especially after what he did."

Charlie could not believe his ears; this friendly, considerate man had treated him as nice as any person he knew. And then he'd confessed in detail to planning the death of another man.

"Wow Jerry, that's quite the story," murmured Charlie. "Do you think Jim has any regrets?"

"If he does it's a mystery to me. He's never come to see me in the hospital or written to me to say he's concerned or sorry. But I'm not worried about how he's feeling. I know how he's going to feel in the future." Jerry gave a half smile. "Well, I have to run—I want to get something from the cafeteria. It's been a pleasure meeting you, Charlie. I'm sure we'll have more chances to talk. I've got some great jokes I'd love to share with you. Take care."

And then there was Harvey, on Charlie's right. Harvey had owned and operated a one-man garage. One day Harvey had a car up on a jack. He was an overly confident man, and he consistently threw caution to the wind. While he was working underneath the car, he put all his strength into trying to remove a rusted-on part. No matter how hard he tried, the part refused to budge. But every time Harvey struggled with his wrenches, the jack would sway, though he ignored this. Finally the jack slipped its hold on the side of the vehicle. The car came down with a crashing sound and pinned Harvey to the floor. He was fortunate that a customer found him so quickly or he would have died. Because of his careless attitude, he'd lost the use of both of his legs. He was now a paraplegic.

Harvey could not get out of his bed. He hadn't followed the instructions regarding changing his sitting position in his wheelchair on a regular basis. As a result he was the proud owner of two good-sized bedsores on his bottom. Paraplegics need to shift their body weight when sitting in their wheelchair. This ensures the circulation to the person's bottom is uniform. Failure to adjust the main point of weight while sitting will result in a bedsore, and bedsores are difficult to heal. Harvey was as incautious about shifting his weight as he had been while working as a mechanic. So now a canopy sat about three feet above his hips in his bed, to keep the sheets from rubbing his exposed sores. While lying in bed he frequently changed his resting position from hip to hip.

On one of the occasions when Harvey was facing Charlie, they got a chance to introduce themselves. Their conversation was pleasant and they both enjoyed chatting and joking with each other. Charlie knew Harvey's story from discussions he'd heard between Harvey and Jerry. Charlie noticed that Harvey's stories changed with each retelling. In one account, the car fell on him because a customer came in and bumped the vehicle, bringing it down on him. Another time a small earth tremor made the car unstable on the jack. It didn't matter that Harvey had a different story each time about how he was injured. What did matter was he didn't seem to accept personal responsibility for being the cause of the accident. It would be difficult for him to move forward when his hold on reality was so slippery.

Anthony never spoke a word; he was an enigma to all the patients. He simply lay in his bed and said nothing, and even if one of his ward mates spoke to him, he refused to respond. When the porters came to take him to physiotherapy, he lay there silently as they got him out of his bed. He wasn't mute, but he might as well have been.

As Charlie thought about his ward mates, he realized that each of them had arrived at their current situation by different circumstances. And each of them had difficulty determining what direction their life should take. Anthony appeared to be content with languishing in bed and doing as little as possible to finding a positive direction in his life. Jerry lived and breathed hatred and it consumed his every thought. His friendly, joke-telling façade was designed to mask his true ambition. Harvey was reluctant about accepting accountability for his accident and his resulting condition. He was unlikely to ever realize that he needed to play a role in deciding where his life was headed. It seemed to Charlie that each of his new friends was stuck, for one reason or another. He wondered if he was stuck. If he was, how was he stuck? Was he unknowingly blocking his chance of moving forward into a new, positive future?

The porters came into the room and transported two of his roommates. They were on their way to physiotherapy. Charlie held high hopes that this therapy would translate into a regeneration of his body and open new avenues in his working life. Time would tell.

Charlie took advantage of every chance available to discuss how other quadriplegics were approaching their search for work, but he didn't get very far. Many of the inpatient and outpatient quadriplegics were unable to identify any jobs available to quadriplegics, and they lived on social assistance programs.

Charlie also talked with both inpatient and outpatient paraplegics and discovered that over 50 percent of them had jobs. They were uniformly more motivated to look for work. Their level of physical limitation didn't hinder them as much from seeking a productive role in their life. One of the most important factors was their higher level of independence. They could drive a vehicle and travel on their own to and from any location. And employers didn't have to meet the same kind of facility requirements when hiring a paraplegic compared to a quadriplegic. As for the other 50 percent of paraplegics Charlie talked to, they seemed content living on social assistance.

Charlie found that the talks he and I had produced the greatest exploration of ideas. I made sure that I got into his room as often as possible to share both his and my aspirations. I was impressed with the three approaches he'd come up with to find work. Identifying areas of personal interest seemed to be the best approach. When we talked about using skills developed as an approach we learned that they all focused on his hobby, working on trucks, or his business, which focused on trucking with some cold-call selling. Charlie had some business administration skills, although Ruth had done all of the business-related paperwork. The last approach the two of us looked at involved key areas of knowledge derived from his public school education and small business owner's seminars. We had a lot of trouble identifying any special knowledge areas that would be transferrable.

Days turned into weeks and weeks turned into months. The occupational training area in the Rehab was unable to custom-fit any tools that would increase Charlie's functionality. During one of my lunch breaks, Charlie and I were looking at his areas of interest.

Charlie started listing them for me: "Truckin', skills required to run a truckin' business, helpin' small business owners get started, runnin' a one man operation, how to extend the life of an asset like a truck, dealin' with customers, how to convert a onetime customer into a long-term customer, sellin' our business to a new customer and customer service."

"That's a great list," I told him. "And you've dealt with people on all kinds of different levels. Something that might work could involve you being a consultant to other truckers. Do you remember seeing any jobs like that?"

"No, I haven't seen any jobs that would be remotely similar to consultin' for truckers."

"What about putting on a seminar like the ones you took? Do you think you could do that?"

Charlie thought for a moment, then looked a little dejected. "All the seminars I went to had a presenter usin' visual aids like overhead projectors and flip charts. Since I don't have the use of my hands, I couldn't use any of those tools. Plus, the presenters walked back and forth across the stage. This helped keep up my interest. I can't move my wheelchair. Me sittin' in one place would get borin' for the audience."

"But all your experience dealing with customers and suppliers and getting new customers—there's got to be some kind of job that uses these skills. We just have to put our heads together and find it."

"Thanks, Don!" Charlie said. "I got to admit I was gettin' discouraged. No matter how hard I looked at our list, nothin' was standin' out for me. But I think you've found at least a possibility. I'm not sure yet what it really means for future jobs, but it's a start."

I looked at my watch. "I have to get back to work. I went overtime on today's lunch break, but it was worth it."

As I walked out of the room, I realized that despite our age difference, Charlie felt like a best friend to me. I also realized that Charlie was smiling. The look of hope in his eyes was a new look and it held a lot of power.

CHAPTER 6
Pathways

The lights were off and Charlie lay in bed. He had committed this evening's session to idea generation. The past two months had been productive. In his evening sessions he had continued to develop interest-based job ideas, although he had discovered some personal pitfalls he needed to avoid. For example, his idea generation worked well only if he refused to dwell on his pre-accident losses. Focusing on his losses blocked all his attempts to create a job list, his future pathway.

But Charlie also made an important discovery: while he needed to accept, release and forget all of his pre-accident losses, it was also crucial for him to hold onto his pre-accident resources. He had acquired extensive business knowledge, developed strong reasoning skills and cultivated excellent interpersonal skills. These resources were key in developing a job list that integrated his interests and his skills.

However, even though he'd committed himself to accepting his new situation, he still had a daily battle on his hands. Charlie found if he had trouble coping with day-to-day events, he would slip into dwelling on his losses. If he stayed centered and handled life as he encountered it, he remained focused on his skills and opportunities. His emotional state became his thought-process gauge.

Charlie really needed to talk about his issues with others, but his roommates didn't make good candidates for such discussions. Whenever Charlie tried to speak to either Jerry or Harvey about job possibilities, without fail each channeled the conversation back to his own situation. This would have been fine except that Jerry's situation revolved around planning to harm his former friend, and Harvey's involved denying any responsibility for his current circumstances.

On the other hand, Charlie valued his talks with Don. He always felt better after they had explored an idea because Don stayed centered on Charlie's opportunity pathway.

… …

A red 1961 Volkswagen Beetle was parked in front of Charlie's three-bedroom bungalow. Don got out and examined Charlie's home, which he was visiting for the first time. A thirty-foot wheelchair ramp ran from the front door threshold to the cement walkway. It looked like a giant wooden tongue sticking out at any anyone walking past his house. Don walked up to the front door. Ruth must have been waiting for him because she opened the door before he could ring the doorbell.

"Hi, Don. Charlie's waiting for you in the backyard."

Don thanked her and headed around the back. Charlie was facing away from him, in the tall-backed wheelchair that had been built to ensure he had full neck support. All that showed from the rear was the wavy crest of Charlie's hair, combed but thinning from lying in bed in the same position for long periods.

"Hi, Charlie," Don said. "How are you doing today?"

"Fine, Don. Come around in front of me so I can see you."

Don picked up a lawn chair and placed it in front of Charlie. Then he sat down and looked around. A combination of flowers and ornamental bushes grew in a soft, curving, almost feminine line that skirted his house and gave the bungalow a settled, cozy feel. From the center of the backyard a twenty-foot Alberta blue spruce rocketed upward. Birdfeeders were strategically placed nearby, providing the birds with safe refuge in the tree. Don watched some small birds dart from the feeder to the tree and back again.

"Black-capped chickadees," said Charlie. "They take the sunflower seeds and then land on a branch in the tree. They hit the seed on a branch to break the shell so they can get the kernel out. Clever, eh?"

The well-fed birds sang their hearts out and filled the air with a symphony of songs.

"I could watch the birds all day," said Charlie. "They're amazin'."

Ruth came out carrying a tray with two glasses on it. She placed the glass with an extra-long bent straw on Charlie's wheelchair tray, then moved a little lawn table next to Don's chair and put his glass down on it.

"Enjoy your drinks, boys," she called out as she walked back to the house.

Charlie turned his gaze to Don. "I've been workin' on a difficult problem, and I'd appreciate your advice."

"I'd be happy to help you in any way I can."

"My problem is similar to other patients in the Rehab Hospital. The accident has resulted in me not havin' the use of my four limbs. As a result, I can't do anythin' for myself or anyone else. I can't walk, feed myself, take care of my personal needs, wheel my chair, get in and out of bed, shake hands, drive, or do anythin' that requires use of my neck or my extremities. I've been asking the physiotherapists if they have any suggestions about possible jobs. When I tell them that my profession was drivin' a truck, they can't seem to give me any ideas." Charlie paused and took a sip from his drink. "I've talked to some of the other quadriplegics," he went on, "and almost all of them were unable to come up with a job either. One patient told me he knew a person that had become an artist, holding brushes in her mouth. Unfortunately, I wouldn't be able to do that because I haven't got any movement of my neck or head."

"Did the patient say whether the artist is someone that lives around here?" Don asked.

"No, he just said that he'd seen a TV show that talked about her and showed some of her work. After I spoke to the patients, I went to the occupational therapy department and asked for their help. They told me they did most of their work with partial quadriplegics, paraplegics, amputees and stroke patients." Charlie let out a sigh. "Don, I feel like I'm completely blocked. It looks like I might end up on welfare. But I couldn't take a life of sittin' in a wheelchair or lyin' in bed all day."

"We're nowhere near that kind of situation, Charlie," Don replied. "I'm sure we'll come up with a job that'll be just right for you."

"I sure hope so, because I feel like I've exhausted all of my avenues. Another area I looked into more was meditation. I hoped by quietin' my mind and emotions, that it'd open my thinkin' processes. I did this for a period of time but it didn't lead to any job ideas. Somethin' else I tried was takin' a more active approach to my evenin' sessions. Every night when the lights were out, I'd focus my mind on an area of interest and try to generate job ideas. But I didn't get anywhere with that either.

"The next thing I tried was prayer. I've been reachin' out to the Holy Spirit and askin' for guidance and assurance. This has led to a genuine strengthenin' of my faith. I feel a renewal in my connection with God, and I felt comforted by the Holy Spirit. I don't know how to explain it, but I've sensed the Holy Spirit's guidance in everything that takes place in my life. This has made me believe I'm on the right track."

Charlie was quiet for a moment as he watched two birds alight on the feeder. Finally he said, "Anyway, I've done most of the talkin', and I want to hear what you have to say."

"Well, it's too bad no one was able to give you some ideas to consider," said Don, shaking his head. "The one thing you mentioned that got me thinking was the quadriplegic artist. I know you've dismissed that idea, but I think you can build on it. You have all kinds of assets, like your business knowledge, your strong reasoning skills, your great interpersonal skills, your mind, your eyes, your ears, your nose, your tongue, your voice and your mouth. You can use these assets as a starting point." Don drained his drink, then pointed at his glass. "Hey, this just gave me a great idea. For example, if you decided you wanted to be a wine taster, you've got the three things you need—your mind, your nose and your tongue!"

"That *is* a great idea," replied Charlie. "I've never even thought about takin' on that type of job."

"Or, given your strong spiritual connection, maybe you could work as a counselor for troubled young people. Or how about being a drug and alcohol abuse counselor, or a 911 operator, or working at a crisis center? And last but not least you could be a career counselor for people with spinal cord injuries."

A long pause followed Don's last statement. A loud crash and some muttered curses shattered the stillness of the air. Charlie was startled and his entire six-foot-four-inch body spasmed involuntarily. He opened his eyes and looked toward the direction of the noise. He couldn't figure out what was going on. He could see the top of someone's head moving up and down, but it wasn't Don. The person was picking up the spilled contents of a breakfast tray. And there were no birds around and no trees. The noise continued and as Charlie listened to it, he realized it was coming from the hallway and he was in his hospital bed. It felt like a giant hiccup in his reality.

He thought for a moment and remembered the orderlies preparing him for bed and turning the lights out. Next he recalled taking time for his evening meditation. As he silently interacted with the Holy Spirit, he knew he had a strong and clear connection. During this period, Charlie drifted off. He knew in his heart that his comforter and guide would help him with his problem. As he collected his thoughts, he remembered discussing his problem with Don in the dream.

Hope flashed through his being as he remembered the suggestions that Don—or was it Don?—had given him. He now had some real possibilities to pursue. A quiet "yee-haw" escaped his lips. He had a loving family, real physical assets and usable job skills, and at least half a dozen areas to explore. What additional training would he need? Which of the ideas that came out in his dream would give him the greatest satisfaction? What other jobs existed that required the assets he had? Until this morning, he had felt like an animal trapped in a maze with no exit.

An orderly came into his room and placed a food tray in front of Anthony. When the man turned around, Charlie could see that it was Don.

"Don, you wouldn't believe the dream I had last night. It was like watching a movie—and you were the main character!"

"Did we have a good time?" Don queried with a smile.

"When you have some free time I'll share the dream with you. It's changed the entire direction in my life."

"Wow!" said Don. "That's a dream worth hearing about."

CHAPTER 7
Parsing

Charlie had trouble believing he would be discharged from the Rehab Hospital the next morning. He smiled when he thought about the people he had met and the friends he had made. Each person had contributed to his evolution, even though they didn't know the important part they had played. The patients had opened up, shared their life-changing experiences, and described how they were dealing with their current situations.

Because of their sharing, Charlie had learned that anger, resentment or depression were barriers to seeing life's opportunities. He had evolved as a person and in his way of looking at life. He discovered the necessity of accepting the impact of his life-altering event. The time he'd spent with his peers, his evening meditation sessions, his discussions with Don and his willingness to be completely honest with himself had helped him forge a winning attitude that equipped him to find a meaningful and satisfying role in his life. He knew that tomorrow would feel like graduation day.

... ...

This afternoon would be the last in-hospital visit that Charlie and I would have together before he was discharged. At 3:45 p.m. I went to Charlie's room. My shift was over so I was wearing my civilian clothing. I got behind Charlie's wheelchair and pushed him to the fourth-floor visiting area. No one else was there, so we could have a completely candid conversation.

I started. "Charlie, you said you had a dream that involved me? I'm really curious to hear about it."

"I've never had a dream like this one, Don! Sometimes, like at the beginnin', I was like an observer, watchin' things unfold the way you watch a movie. Then at other times I was *in* the movie. For instance, I watched you drive your red Beetle up to the front of my house, even though I had my back turned to you. After you sat down, we started talkin'. I told you that I had spoken to physiotherapists, occupational therapists and fellow quadriplegics. None had any suggestions except for one of my fellow quadriplegics. He mentioned he knew a quadriplegic who had become an artist usin' a paintbrush in her teeth. I know I can't do this because of my restricted neck mobility. Then I asked you if you had any suggestions."

"And did I?" I asked.

"You sure did. First, though, you told me that I had more usable assets. First you listed, all the things we've talked about in the past, like my business skills and such. But this time you also pointed out that I had my mind, my eyes, my ears, my nose, my tongue, my mouth and my voice."

At this point Charlie's face grew animated. "Then you suggested I consider careers that would use any or all of my assets. Some of the ideas you came up with were a wine taster, a 911 operator, a crisis center adviser, a drug and alcohol counselor, a counselor for troubled youth, and you even suggested a career that doesn't exist as far as I know: career counselin' for quadriplegics. So that sums up my dream. Since you played a starrin' role in it, I thought you'd find it interestin'. What d'you think?"

"That's a pretty impressive dream," I said. I sat back in my chair and thought for a moment. "Charlie, I'm thinking you tapped into something special in your dream. You might have received real spiritual guidance. Those all sound like pretty good ideas—but you're the only one who can decide how much each idea appeals to you. Do you want us to go over them together?"

"That'd be great, Don. It'll give me a runnin' start."

"All right, let's begin with the wine taster."

Charlie grinned. "I love both red and white wine. I'm not sure how you go about gettin' into that area but that's a definite yes."

"Great! We've started on a real positive note." I watched Charlie's legs; they were spasming. This often happened when he'd been sitting in his chair too long. "Charlie, we'd better do this review quickly, because I can tell by your body actions that you need to rest on your bed for a while."

"Sure, that's fine with me, although I have to tell you I find this whole process excitin' as hell."

"All right, another one you mentioned from the dream was a 911 operator."

"The only concern I have with that is the unpredictability of my whole-body spasms," said Charlie, frowning. "I'd be afraid that I'd lock up physically, which includes my hearin' and my voice. If that happened I might mess up a call and put someone's life in jeopardy."

"Ok, we'll put the 911 job as a maybe," I replied. "There might be something that can be done to get your body spasms under control."

"One of the other jobs you suggested in the dream was bein' a counselor for troubled youth. I like this idea because I enjoy workin' with young people. What do you think about this one?"

"I guess you'd need to look into what organizations exist that offer counseling to teenagers. I've heard of a few, and they're all pretty specific. For example, there's one that helps runaway kids, another one for pregnant teenagers and so on. So first you'd have to figure out what area appeals to you, then you'd need to find out what kind of training's required. I bet you'd do well in this type of job, because you're smart and kind and you're good with people."

Charlie smiled. "Thanks, Don. So I'll keep it on the 'maybe' list."

"Okay. Next?"

"One of the other jobs mentioned in my dream was a drug and alcohol counselor."

Now this was an area I knew a bit about. "Charlie," I said, "a guy I know told me that his friends use the rehab system to avoid jail time. Apparently the courts look at a person getting counseling as less likely to offend down the road. The only problem is, my friend said the guys that do this have no intention of changing their ways. They're just using the system. I think you'd find it frustrating working with people that aren't serious about changing."

"Yeah, you're right." Charlie looked thoughtful. "I'd want clients that are totally committed to recoverin' from their addictions. Otherwise, what's the point? So I don't think this job would be a good fit for me."

"I understand. Are there any other jobs left on your list?"

"There's one I'm really interested in—crisis center adviser. Do you know anythin' about that?"

I did know a little, because my mother, the psychiatric nurse, had a friend who volunteered at the crisis center in Winnipeg. "I'm pretty sure most of the crisis center intervention is done on the telephone, Charlie. People having serious problems usually call a crisis center helpline. I think—but I'm not certain about this—that the crisis center here in the city also does some work in counseling facilities. But I bet you need specialized training because you could be dealing with some heavy stuff. And you'd need the place to be wheelchair accessible."

"If telephone contact is the only method of functionin' as a crisis center adviser, I'd have to put a question mark beside this one, Don." Charlie looked a little disappointed. "I'd probably run into the same trouble I worried I could have as a 911 operator. But if there *was* crisis intervention work bein' done in a facility, I'd be very interested in lookin' into this job."

"That's great—you have another 'maybe.' Anything else?"

"Yeah, and this is the last one. It's a complete unknown to me. It involves quadriplegic career counsellin.'"

"I've never heard of that," I said. "If it existed, surely we'd have someone here at Rehab doing it." But I found myself growing excited. "That's an unusual career idea, Charlie. Since it doesn't seem to exist, the unknowns are almost limitless. Like with the other jobs, you'd need to find out what kind of training you'd need. And then, I wonder, would it be your own business? Or would you work, say, at a hospital like this one?" "It could go either way," said Charlie, and I could see the wheels turning. "Or maybe at job agency and you'd specialize in quadriplegic job placement?" I paused. This job was trickier because we had to make it up as we went along. "I'm just throwing ideas out there. I don't know if I'm on the right track."

"No, you're being a tremendous help, Don. I think this job would be very interestin', even with all its uncertainties. I'll put this one on the 'strong maybe' list."

"That's great, Charlie! So we've got a 'yes' for wine taster, a 'maybe' beside the 911 operator and a 'no' beside the drug and alcohol counselor. The remaining 'maybe's include a youth counselor for troubled teens, a crisis center adviser and a quadriplegic career counselor. That's interesting. Your 'maybe' list leans almost entirely to counseling or helping others. Now I can see why you and I are close friends. My goal in life is to find a career that involves helping others, and it appears your goal's the same."

"That's amazin', Don. I like how you took the 'maybe' parts and created a whole picture. I'm real glad we've had this chance to talk about possible jobs for me, and I want you to know how much I appreciate all your input." Charlie was practically beaming. "I'll need to consider what you've said when I'm evaluatin' each of the job opportunities. Now I'd appreciate it if you'd take me back to my room. I've got a lot to think about so I can figure out what steps to take next."

I smiled back at my friend. "I'm real glad I could help. If you decide you want to talk about this or anything else, I'm around."

I got behind the tall-backed wheelchair and pushed it toward Charlie's room. Each of us was lost in thought. Charlie was thinking about being discharged from the Rehab Hospital tomorrow. He was also trying to decide which of the jobs he'd investigate first. I was visualizing myself in a line of work that would see me providing career guidance to others. Both of us had gained from sharing Charlie's dream. Both of us were on a meaningful quest of our own.

CHAPTER 8
Crossroads

It was a cold Wednesday afternoon. I had just finished my daytime work shift and completed my report to the evening shift. In my report, I mentioned that the patient in bed one, Room 406, was seriously depressed. I recommended that both the evening and the night shift keep a close eye on him. I left the fourth floor and made my way down to the orderlies' locker room. I peeled off my stiff, starched white shirt and pants. I welcomed the loose comfort of my blue jeans and sweater.

Wednesdays were days that I looked forward to, because it was the day of the week that I went to visit Charlie in his home. He'd been out of the hospital for over a month. In the six months Charlie had been in the rehab unit, he'd been unable to gain any use of his arms, hands or legs. The only function that had improved involved his breathing. In the early phase of his recovery, the doctors had been uncertain if he would be able to breathe independently or if he would need assistance. A combination of the healing achieved on the Stryker unit plus work done in physiotherapy had improved his situation to the point that he could breathe on his own.

Charlie was in the midst of reading a book when I walked into his living room. Ruth had purchased a book holder designed to display two pages at a time. Whenever they were sitting in the living room together, Ruth would reach over and turn the pages for him. He looked up and a broad smile spread across his face. We had become best friends because of the many hours of visiting and going out to events together. Since we both enjoyed hockey, this was where we often ended up.

I drew one of the living room chairs close to Charlie and asked, "How are you and the family doing?"

"The family's doin' well and the adjustment to livin' at home has been pretty easy. How are things goin' at the Rehab?"

"Things are going well at work. This afternoon we received three new patients from the General Hospital. It kept us hopping to get them admitted and straightened away before our shift change. All three were in their early twenties, all males and all paraplegics. Drinking and driving were the cause of their injuries."

I had a clear sense that I was under Charlie's scrutiny. "Well," he finally said, "When are you gonna tell me what has you lookin' so concerned?"

"Is it that obvious?"

"It's obvious to me because you and I've become close. We've spent a lot of time talkin' so I can sense now when somethin's going on with you."

"Well, something happened at the rehab unit today and I don't know what to do. I've never gone through anything like this and I can't think about anything else. The problem is, it involves a patient and, as you know, I can't discuss patient details outside the hospital."

"I can tell it's botherin' you. I've been out the Rehab for some time now, so it's unlikely that I'd be able to guess who you're talking about. You don't have to tell me who it is. If you talk in a general way, you wouldn't be violatin' the Rehab's rules. Plus you know that anythin' you tell me doesn't go any further than here."

I took some time to think about it and decided Charlie was right. A lot of patients had come and gone since he'd been discharged. It would be virtually impossible for him to tell who I was talking about. And I needed to talk to someone about the situation, and I trusted Charlie more than anyone else.

"I was helping one of my patients with his morning preparations and he asked me to do something that shook me up. Until this morning his progress had been pretty positive. He seemed to be making headway in his treatment programs. The only thing staff had noted was that he was somewhat withdrawn. He just didn't seem to want to talk much, either to staff or to other patients. Other than that, there wasn't anything to indicate a problem. I think that's why I nearly fell over when he asked if I would, as he put it, 'simply push him down a flight of stairs.' He said if I did that, he'd die, and he promised to give me his entire bank savings, ten thousand dollars."

I stopped here and stared at the floor.

Charlie could tell I was feeling troubled, because he said gently, "It's okay, Don…Go on."

I looked into Charlie's kind brown eyes and continued, though it was hard to do. "I hated myself for the next thing I did. I figured out that his offer was equal to three years' income for me." I shuddered as I recounted this to Charlie. An image of this man tumbling down the stairs flashed into my mind, as well as other stark images of death or near-death that were now embedded in my consciousness, such as the woman who saw her husband decapitated, and Charlie's truck hitting the bridge.

"Well, now I know why you're upset. What are you gonna do?"

"I don't know. There are a bunch of things bothering me. First, I must have given it serious thought at some level, because I did the math. Second, I reported his state of mind, but not his offer, to the incoming shift. I just told them he seemed depressed. The third thing is I don't know what to do when I deal with this patient again. I made the required 'watch' report to the evening and night staff, but this whole thing still troubles me. I don't feel I've done enough."

I got up and began to pace a bit across the living room. "The Rehab's goal is to help our clients find new meaning in their very changed lives. As a staff member, that's my job. But it's clear that the man in room 406 isn't searching for a new future—he's given up all hope. The choice he wants to make is a complete waste of his potential, and it's so drastic, so permanent."

I stopped pacing and sat down again opposite Charlie.

"It's hard to stand by and watch someone else in severe emotional pain, isn't it?" Charlie looked intently into my eyes as he replied.

He always said that the eyes were the portals to the soul. Back then I'd never fully understood the meaning of this statement, but I certainly do now. "Hard? More than hard. I felt like I should be sounding the alarms and restraining this guy so he wouldn't hurt himself. Instead, I walked out of his room murmuring that life *is* worth living and then I made a 'watch' footnote on his file."

Charlie wore a look of deep compassion. "Each of us invests ourselves in somethin'," he began softly. "For me it was expandin' my trucking business by one more eighteen-wheeler within a twelve-month period. My investment had two main parts to it: my body and my money. When I became a quadriplegic I lost all of those options and a lot of my freedom of choice. At first my main battle focused on my body, because I felt like it had betrayed me and let me down. It took a long time for me to realize that my body wasn't to blame and that it was doin' the best job it could. I began to realize that I'd made choices that had led up to my accident, and I had to take responsibility for those choices."

"What do you mean, Charlie? What kind of choices?" I asked.

"There's a reason I fell asleep at the wheel. I was puttin' my business ahead of everythin' else in my life and workin' ridiculous hours, pushin' my body beyond what it was really capable of. Until I accepted responsibility for that, I wouldn't be able to deal with the depression and anger—and the loss of hope. The isolation I felt was awful, and I wasn't able to hear my spiritual guiding voice as long as I hung onto all that negative stuff."

At that moment Ruth came into the living room carrying a tray with two coffee cups and a straw. Looking from Charlie to me, and realizing we were deep in serious conversation, she just smiled and placed the tray between us. Charlie thanked her and she silently left the room.

"I remember lyin' in bed one night," Charlie continued, "and realizin' that my body hadn't betrayed me. I'd accepted a lie. The truth was that I wasn't seekin' out the opportunities available to me. I had to seek them out and then figure out which ones offered me the most fulfillment. The night I accepted this truth and lay quietly in bed and opened my heart for more guidance, well, that night I found a new peace, a new sense of self-worth. I admitted my part in my current situation and asked for help."

As Charlie paused, I put the straw in his cup of coffee and helped him take a sip of his drink.

"You see, I was angry because I felt cheated and betrayed. My dreams, my hopes, my image of myself and my idea of personal worth required complete rethinkin'. Do you remember me mentionin' once that I had to live a 'faith fall life'?"

"Yes," I said, "and I've been hoping you'd tell me what you meant."

"When I was plannin' on expandin' my trucking business, I went to a leadership course. The instructor had five of us come up on stage. Another five people that none of us knew came up and stood behind each one of us. We weren't supposed to look behind us at any time durin' this exercise. The leader told the five front people to fall backward into the hands of the five people behind. He called this a 'faith fall,' a fall that trusted an unseen person to catch us. We all did what the instructor said. I was frightened placin' my safety, my well-bein' in the hands of an unknown, unseen, person. It was a lesson in extendin' your trust beyond yourself. I'll never forget the helpless feelin' of fallin' backward, prayin' that someone would catch me. So I remembered that experience the night I lay in bed and took responsibility for my role in my current situation. Once I'd accepted this truth, it was like I was released and could finally move forward. I asked for divine guidance in my new circumstances. I decided that no matter what happened I'd live a 'faith fall life'—I'd fall unconditionally into the Holy Spirit's hands and trust Him to catch me and hold me up."

Charlie cleared his throat and I held the straw to his lips for a sip of coffee. "That guy in room 406 has a battle ahead of him. He's standin' at his crossroads and he's got a lot of things he has to decide and accept before he can move on from the depression he's battlin'. All you can do, Don, is offer him your concern, your interest and your carin' support. These things might not feel like a lot to you, but they'll mean a lot to him. He's confessed his deepest feelings to you. The fact that you continue to believe in him and encourage him, well, that's a real powerful, positive act."

As Charlie finished speaking, I noticed a copy of the "Serenity Prayer," a masterpiece of framed truth, hanging on the wall behind him. We had one in our house when I was growing up too. As I read its familiar words—"God grant me the serenity to accept the things I cannot change; courage to change the things I can; and the wisdom to know the difference"—I knew in my heart that Charlie's words concerning my patient were also framed in truth. I felt the inner peace that divine truth always brings to my heart.

I put my hand on Charlie's arm and held the straw to his lips again. "Charlie, I can always count on you being straight with me. I sure appreciate that." At the same time, I thanked God for giving me this wonderful resource in my quest for meaning.

CHAPTER 9
The Library

Charlie found himself waiting outside a large, ornately carved wooden door in a long corridor with a high ceiling. There was no name plate attached to the outside of the door, so as he waited he tried to remember the name of the person he'd come to see. But no matter how hard he tried, all he drew was a blank. He tried some of his memory tricks to see if they'd stir his sluggish memory. Still nothing. He gave up trying to remember the person's name and began thinking about the questions he'd ask. He'd learned from previous meetings that he needed to have questions prepared so he could take full advantage of the opportunity.

What was this person's area of expertise? If he could recall this, he could optimize his questions and explore his or her knowledge base. He still had a lot of information blanks involving some of the jobs left on his list. He wondered if this person would have some future influence on his academic education, skill training or job placement. His mind slipped back to all the unknowns related to this meeting. How did he end up waiting outside this door? Who had brought him to this meeting? The uncertainty started a mild panic attack. As he worked on settling his nerves down, his attention was drawn to the door.

The door knob made a small clicking sound as it rotated, indicating that the occupant was about to appear. A tall, slender man opened the door and said, "Good morning, Charlie. My name is Peter. I will help you into my library. I've been looking forward to meeting you."

As Charlie entered Peter's library, he was struck by what he saw: all the walls were book-covered shelves that ran from the floor to a twelve-foot ceiling. Although Peter's desk was tidy, it was covered with piles of slender manila folders. As Charlie looked at Peter, he noticed that his eyes were bright and clear. He gave the impression of being intelligent and knowledgeable. He had a neatly trimmed silver beard, and his hair was white, wavy and combed straight back. An old pair of gold-rimmed glasses suggested that fashion was not high on his list of priorities.

Peter studied Charlie, and Charlie felt as if the older man had looked right through him.

"Charlie," said Peter, "I understand that you're working your way through a number of career options. I would appreciate you telling me what opportunities you are considering."

Taken aback, Charlie paused for a moment. He'd expected an open exchange of ideas and thoughts, but the way this had started it looked as though Peter planned on interviewing him. He decided that he'd respond to the questions but he'd guide the interview into a discussion. "I began by identifying the assets I have. They're as follows: I have extensive business knowledge, strong reasonin' skills, strong interpersonal skills, and my mind, my eyes, my ears, my voice, my tongue and my mouth. So I started with a list of jobs that'd use these assets. For instance, a wine taster, a 911 operator, a crisis center counselor, a counselor that works with troubled teens, and last but not least is workin' with quadriplegics as a life and career counselor. I need to find out what existing services are out there, what type of additional trainin' I'd need, and in the case of a 911 operator, I need to see if my body spasms can be stopped. I know I have to move forward on these job opportunities, but I feel confused and stuck."

Peter sat back, his elbows resting on the arms of the chair, his fingers intertwined in front of him. Charlie studied Peter's hands as he waited for his response. They were the hands of a man who'd done hard physical labor. The fingers were swollen, the skin worn and etched with lines. Peter pressed his fingers to his lips, and a crease formed in his forehead. He appeared to be considering what he would say next. Finally he began to speak.

"Charlie, I'm impressed. In my opinion, you've made admirable progress in defining your assets and creating a list of possible jobs. But it's normal to be having difficulty dealing with a life-changing event like yours. Many give up and live a life filled with frustration, anger and loss of meaning.

I'm sure many of the things I'm about to say will seem obvious to you because you have lived with them. But there's a good reason for my saying them—it will help set the stage for additional comments I want to make. When you were first injured, I'm sure it felt as if you were living in a dream, and if you could just wake up you'd find you had your previous life back. As time went on, you began to realize that the injuries you had suffered were not going away, and the life you had trained for, planned for and in which you'd invested time and energy, no longer existed.

As you lay in bed recovering, you began to see that many of the things you used to do were no longer possible. Each one of these things felt like a loss. Every day you realized there were a growing number of losses. As if that were not enough, you had to deal with a dark, suffocating depression. You went through a period where you even questioned your self-worth. How could your family love you in this condition? Compared to before, you had so little you could do and offer them. Each session of physiotherapy was a struggle. Everything you investigated ended up being a dead end. How could you fit into a new life that had no shape, no meaning?"

Peter paused and, opening one of the manila folders on his desk, briefly studied its contents. Inwardly Charlie marveled at how this stranger could have such insight into his life. Then Peter started to speak again.

"Slowly but steadily you began to see that others valued you. As you saw your value through their eyes, you began to see the value of others in your life. You battled and rejected the depression that sought to paralyze you. You continued to struggle to improve on the physical and intellectual assets you had. You didn't wait for someone to come and lead you. You searched for ways to be productive. You looked for meaning where others saw none. You used evening sessions to strengthen your connection with the Holy Spirit, and He's been faithful in providing you with guidance. This should be your first and most important asset, a solid spiritual connection and foundation."

Peter put the manila folder neatly back onto one of the piles and smiled warmly. "Charlie, you rose above your life-changing event. You are able to overcome adversity and redefine yourself. This should be your second asset. This is the one common challenge for all people facing a life-changing event: they have to redefine their lives to include their new abilities. They must also resist the common enemy, depression. It blinds them and makes their attempts to move forward more difficult. Few of us realize there is a spirit in each one of us. You have a fighting spirit that supports you in all your endeavors. This is your third asset.

So now you have twelve assets: a solid spiritual connection, the gift of overcoming adversity, a fighting spirit, extensive business knowledge, solid reasoning skill, strong interpersonal skills, your mind, your eyes, your ears, your tongue, your voice and your mouth. This asset base prepares you for any task. Have I left out anything in my summary of your experiences and your assets?"

Charlie smiled back. "No, you've done an excellent job of reviewin' how I got to this point. You also pointed out three important assets that I didn't take into account. But I'm still having a hard time with something. See, in my case, I was used to being big and strong and independent; I went all over the country and had friends everywhere. Then I lost my mobility, my freedom and my friends. My world consisted of the hospital, and my outside connections were reduced to my family's visits on weekends. And now I depend on others for every aspect of my livin'. I still find it hard to ask for help."

I'm glad you mentioned that. Everyone has issues specific to their situation that they need to deal with. Your experience in these areas gives you a unique awareness of those problems. Now, when you were describing your assets and the types of work you were considering, were you looking for a job so you could be productive?"

"Of course—bein' productive is my main motivation. Why d'you ask?"

"Being productive is an important aspect of life. Every person needs to feel they're making a contribution. Nevertheless, productivity in itself is just one aspect of what a job can offer you. You're a lucky man. You have the opportunity to do two additional things. You get to choose a job that is meaningful *and* that fulfills your mission in life."

Charlie's brow furrowed. "I'm not sure I understand. If I get a job that uses my assets, isn't that meaningful?"

Peter nodded and stroked his neat beard. "That's a good question. But what has meaning for one person does not have meaning for another. For many people, a job is a way of being productive and earning a salary. That is sufficient meaning for them. Some people find meaning in a job title. The title satisfies a psychological need to be recognized and they assume it infers worth. Or a job may satisfy a need for power. But this does not add extra meaning to the tasks that need to be performed.

But in your case, you need more than just a job to perform. You need to ask yourself some important questions." Peter now leaned forward and looked intently at Charlie. "The first question is, what is my mission in life? You need to identify the direction that meets your deepest internal purpose and that completes you as a person. That will bring a sense of wholeness to your life. The second question is, what job will produce a sense of meaning in my life? The third question is, what assets or knowledge do I have that will help or enrich the lives of others?"

Charlie realized that he was sitting there with his mouth ajar. He had come into Peter's library intending to ask him which jobs he thought Charlie should consider and where someone with his specialized needs could get training. Now he faced a completely new set of considerations. These questions went straight to Charlie's inner core. He knew they were talking about the place that made his existence possible, his inner being. What did Charlie believe would bring meaning to his life? What did Charlie have that could enrich other people's lives? What was his mission in life? Peter hadn't made this process simpler. He had made it much more complex.

Peter looked at Charlie and said kindly, "I know I've given you a lot to think about. I've also given you some new terminology to work with: 'your mission in life' and 'the meaning in your work' and 'enriching the lives of others.' I think I can help you get comfortable with this terminology if I put it in context. I'll share my life story with you, and it may help you focus your thoughts.

When I was a young man, I did jobs that involved hard physical labor. I worked long, difficult days using my hands to lift and carry the products of my work. Unlike you, I didn't have to deal with a life-changing physical injury. Nevertheless, I went through a life-changing event. It resulted in my having a different way of looking at life. One day I listened to a man talking to a group of people. He sounded like a storyteller and his words went right to the core of my being. After listening to him I realized that I'd experienced a deeply personal change in what I considered important and meaningful."

For the first time in my life, I didn't care about money. I no longer sought the approval of others. Instead, I was concerned about the well-being of those I met. I stopped doing the work I'd done all my life, and I began traveling and talking to groups in every city or town. I wanted them to be as happy and fulfilled as I was. My mission in life opened up before me like a rose in full blossom. I wanted to share what I had learned so that others would experience the enrichment and fulfillment that I had. I got tremendous satisfaction when I saw others' lives enriched with what I had learned. Their eyes came alive and they were filled with joy."

Charlie's face beamed with excitement and he exclaimed, "Yee-haw! I think I understand what you're sayin'. Like you, I'd worked my whole life doin' hard physical work as a truck driver. Like you, I had a life-changin' experience with my injury. Like you, I now have knowledge and understandin' of what people go through when they have a life-changin' event. Like you, I can take this knowledge to other people and help them. So that means my mission in life is to work with people who've gone through life-changing events and help them find new meanin' and overcome the barriers that stand in their way. And that's what'll bring meanin' to *my* life—celebratin' with each person that overcomes their situation. Peter, thank you for your help. You've removed the clouds from my eyes. I've now got a meaningful and excitin' direction for my life, beyond my wildest hopes."

Then Charlie's head jolted with a whole-body spasm. For a moment, he didn't know where he was. He looked straight ahead and saw that he was sitting in front of the picture window in his living room. All that had transpired was a dream—or was it? It didn't matter if it was a dream or not. Charlie was now a man with a mission, a man who knew and understood what would bring meaning into his daily life. The excitement that ran though him literally made his entire body vibrate.

Epilogue

Two and a half years had gone by and Charlie had completed all his training. A series of interviews had resulted in him getting a job with an organization dedicated to helping people struggling with life-changing events. The organization had created a new position for Charlie. They felt he should apply his unique insights in a newly created job.

Charlie was now sitting in his high-back wheelchair on the ramp from his house, waiting to be picked up. I drove up and parked on the other side of the street. Charlie's face lit up with the biggest grin I'd ever seen.

"What are you doin' here? You're supposed to be at work this mornin'!"

"Well, Charlie, there's no way I was going to miss this, so I arranged at work to come in late. This is an important day, your first day on the job. Congratulations, my friend."

Ruth was standing next to the wheelchair; a tear of joy ran down her cheek. A noise behind me caught my attention. It was the transport vehicle waiting by the curb ready to take Charlie to work.

This was a day of new beginnings. It was a day that would see my friend the victor over circumstance. This day he would begin working with people battling life-changing experiences. He would help lead them through the doorway of change, and they would travel into a life filled with meaning, with hope.

As Charlie rolled down the wheelchair ramp toward the transport, I wondered—was this a dream, or a dream come true?

Afterword

Most of the story you have just read was inspired by a real person who became a quadriplegic, and whom I had the privilege of caring for as a certified nursing orderly in the Manitoba Rehabilitation Hospital. An exciting and fulfilling career for disabled people is well within the realms of possibility. There are thousands of Charlies alive and well in this world who have carved out significant and successful careers. They have succeeded because they have persisted and persevered. Outlined below are the stories of two highly successful individuals who have overcome their disabilities. The World Health Organization estimates that there are at least 100 million people on the globe who are moderately to severely disabled. I am one of them, and it has been my pleasure to write this book to bring hope and inspiration to the "World's Largest Minority—disABLED People."

The Right Honourable Steven Fletcher

Steven Fletcher worked as an engineer in the mining industry and became a quadriplegic when his automobile struck a moose and broke his neck. He is paralyzed from the neck down and has lost the use of his legs, arms and hands. Steven decided he would go back to university where he obtained a Master's in business administration.

He was elected to the Canadian House of Commons in 2004 in the riding of Winnipeg West. After a successful term as the Opposition critic on health, he was re-elected in 2006, 2008 and 2011. Mr. Fletcher was appointed Minister of State (Transport) following his 2011 re-election. For a more complete list of his impressive accomplishments visit his website at **http://www.stevenfletcher.ca/**.

Professor Stephen Hawking

Internationally renowned physicist Stephen Hawking was referred by his family doctor to a specialist shortly after his twenty-first birthday, and soon after it was confirmed that he had ALS (Lou Gehrig's disease). Stephen Hawking's case is unusual in that he has lived far longer than most people with ALS. He went on to marry, have a family, advance his education and become a full-fledged professor at Cambridge University in Britain. He has published numerous articles and best-selling books.

In 1985 Stephen got pneumonia and lost his ability to speak and make presentations. Undaunted by this obstacle, he had a special device made involving a computer and a voice synthesizer, which helps him to communicate. After three decades with ALS, Stephen Hawking is an excellent example of persevering to overcome severe limitations. For more information please refer to his website at **http://www.hawking.org.uk/**.

Acknowledgements

I did not realize how many people would become involved during the eleven years it took to write this book. First, I want to give all of the honor and the glory to God and thank Him for the continuous inspiration I received while writing this book. It would never have reached completion without the involvement of the following people: Thanks to Dr. C. Bates, Dr. J. Barabtarlo and Dr. J. Rice for playing a key role in sustaining my health and making it possible for me to write; thanks to my parents, Bill and Florence Davis, and to Katherine Speirs for your constant encouragement; thanks to my family and friends for your interest and support; thanks to my editor, Marie-Lynn Hammond, for her untiring dedication to the refinement of this book; my thanks to photographer Mario Hains for giving us permission to use his photo on the front book cover; and thanks to FriesenPress Publishing for getting behind my first book.